THE White Ox

The Journey of Emily Swain Squires

DAN BURR | **RUTH HAILSTONE**

CALKINS CREEK
Honesdale, Pennsylvania

The White Ox started out as my master's thesis at Syracuse University in 2003. Many people helped me turn this great story into a picture book: Murray Tinkelman, John Thompson, Bob Dacey, and William Low. I want to thank them for their wisdom and guidance.

To my sweet daughter, Hannah, for being the model for most of the paintings; Ruth Hailstone for adapting the story; my wife, Patti, for her helpful eye for detail, making sure all the images were consistent and accurate (I also thank her for enduring the many months and years it took me to finish the paintings); Carma de Jong Anderson for her historical honesty; and Emily Swain Squires for her faith and courage.

For Patti —*D.B.*

I want to thank, first of all, my dear husband, Todd, who bore with me and carried me through every step; my angel children—Mary, Jane, Daniel, Esther, Jasmine, Joseph, Samuel, and Heidi; my sweet sister Mary Woodruff, who first presented the opportunity for writing this book; the amazingly talented and patient Dan Burr, who brought the story to life; Carolyn P. Yoder for her wonderful insights and perseverance; my loving parents, Mary and Larry Hill; my brilliant and supportive friends, Janine Bolon, Kim Simmerman, Janele Williams, and Gaylene Hatch; and especially Emily Swain Squires for her legacy of courage and love.

For my mother and her mother —*R.H.*

Text copyright © 2009 by Ruth Hailstone
Illustrations copyright © 2009 by Dan Burr
For information about permission to reproduce selections from this book,
please contact permissions@highlights.com.
Printed in China
Designed by Helen Robinson
First edition
First Boyds Mills Press paperback edition, 2011

Library of Congress Cataloging-in-Publication Data
Hailstone, Ruth.
The white ox : the journey of Emily Swain Squires / Ruth Hailstone ;
illustrations by Dan Burr.
p. cm.
ISBN: 978-1-59078-555-3 (hc) • ISBN: 978-1-59078-897-4 (pb)
1. Squires, Emily Swain, 19th cent. 2. Mormon women—United States—
Biography. 3. Mormon women—England—Biography. I. Burr, Dan. II. Title.

BX8695.S765H35 2009
289.3092—dc22
[B]

2008024154

10 9 8 7 6 5 4 3 2 1 (hc)
10 9 8 7 6 5 4 3 2 1 (pb)

CALKINS CREEK
An Imprint of Boyds Mills Press, Inc.
815 Church Street
Honesdale, Pennsylvania 18431

THE WHITE OX

foreword

In 1830 the Church of Jesus Christ of Latter-day Saints (commonly called Mormons) was organized in Fayette, New York, under the direction of Joseph Smith. Its membership set out to establish Zion, a name used by many religions for a gathering place where God's people live together in peace and community.

The saints (church members) found themselves unwelcome in several states and suffered much persecution. Joseph Smith and his brother Hyrum were murdered for their beliefs in 1844. Finally, the saints were driven from their homes in Illinois and led by Brigham Young across the plains where they settled the Great Salt Lake Valley in 1847.

Emily Swain Squires's parents joined this church in England in 1853, a few months after she was born. Emily was baptized when she was eight years old.

Two years later, Emily, able to sail for half fare, traveled with two fellow Mormons, Brother and Sister Kirby, from Dover, England, to Salt Lake City, Utah Territory, to stay with her uncle John and aunt Sarah in Zion. Her family would join her there a few years later.

At the time, America was torn apart, fighting the Civil War.

This is the true story of Emily Swain Squires, my great-great-grandmother. —R.H.

Emily stood tall and straight, her reflection steady and bold. "Mother says I was so tiny at birth, I would fit in a teacup," she mused to her little sister, Martha.

Martha laughed. "I wish I could go to Zion with you."

"When the biscuit tin is filled with shillings, Mother will bring you and John to Salt Lake, too. By then, this new dress and shoes will be too small for me, and I'll give them to you."

Each morning, Mother prepared sausage, and oatmeal with currants. But today there were scones and jam and a piece of cheese. "Maybe there will be enough to eat around here after you leave," John said, winking.

Over and over again, Emily whispered the words, "I am going to Zion. I am going to Zion."

The *Antarctic* jerked as it pulled from the harbor. Emily clutched the railing, her eyes fixed on England until it became a speck in the blue water. Everything had happened so quickly—the packing, the trip from Dover, even the good-byes.

"Come," said Sister Kirby, "we must find our cots."

Emily spooned the green scum off the drinking water and ladled another cupful. Over half the passengers were terribly ill with measles, including Sister Kirby. Emily wondered how she and the others who were well could care for all the sick.

ot and nauseous, Emily stepped on deck into the cold air. From the stern she watched the water spew from the ship and felt the miles between her and England grow. A sudden gust caught her hat and sent it tumbling into the choppy waves, floating toward home. "Take me with you," Emily whispered.

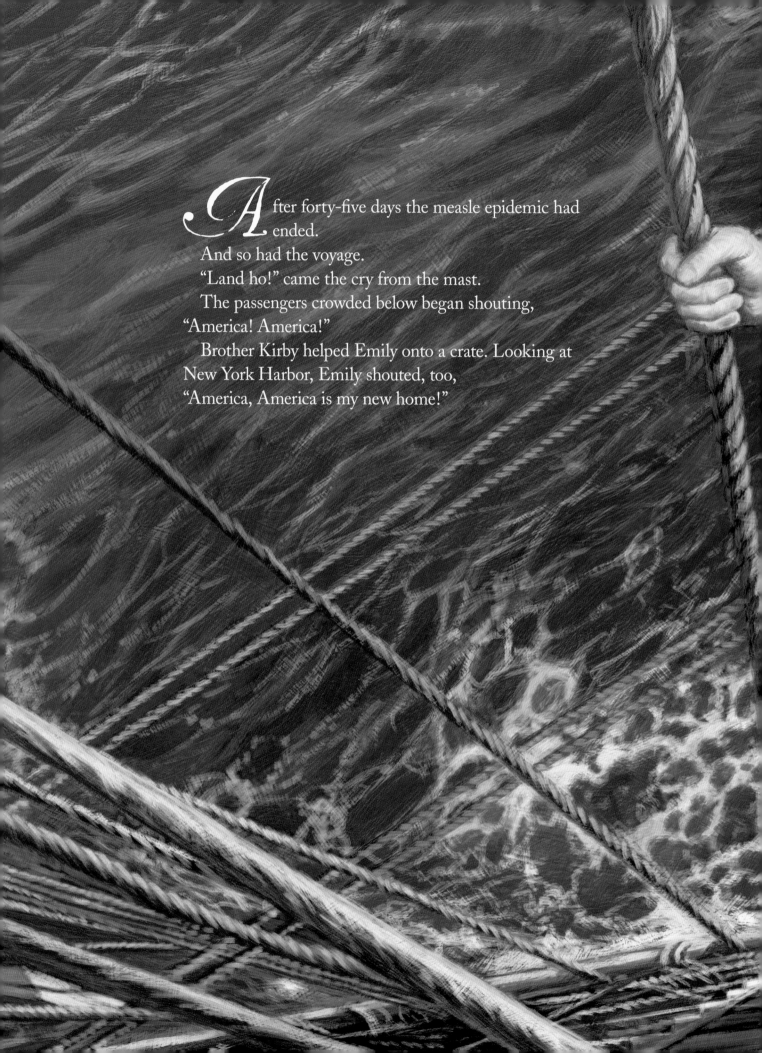

After forty-five days the measle epidemic had ended.

And so had the voyage.

"Land ho!" came the cry from the mast.

The passengers crowded below began shouting, "America! America!"

Brother Kirby helped Emily onto a crate. Looking at New York Harbor, Emily shouted, too, "America, America is my new home!"

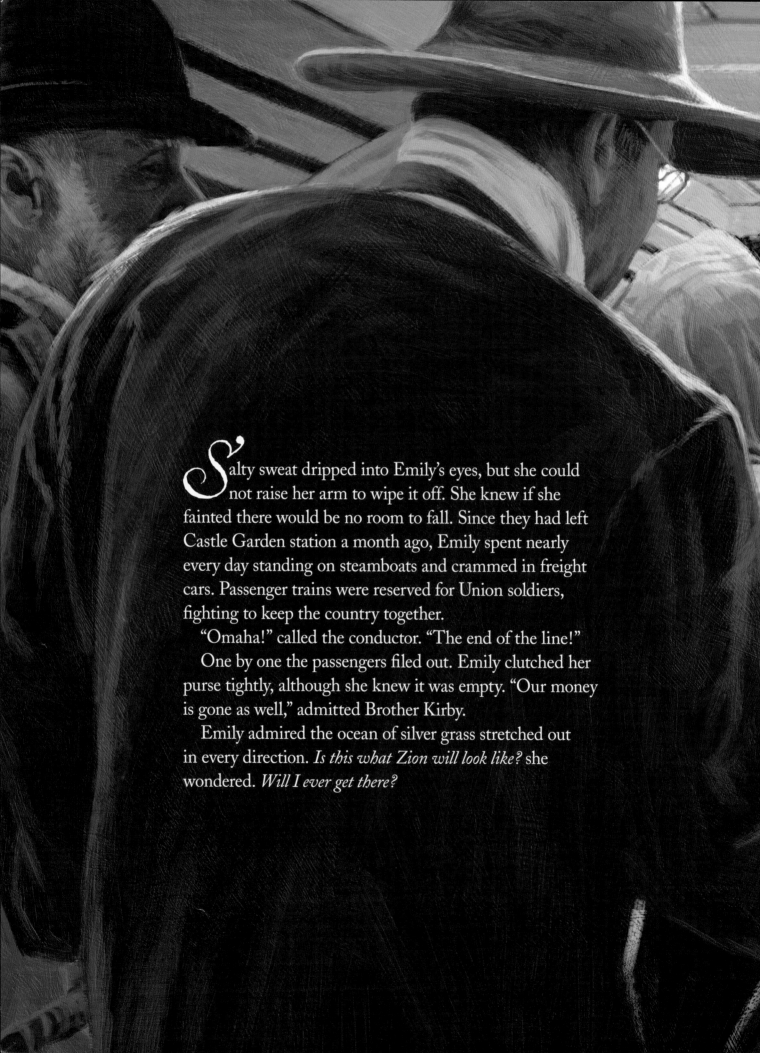

Salty sweat dripped into Emily's eyes, but she could not raise her arm to wipe it off. She knew if she fainted there would be no room to fall. Since they had left Castle Garden station a month ago, Emily spent nearly every day standing on steamboats and crammed in freight cars. Passenger trains were reserved for Union soldiers, fighting to keep the country together.

"Omaha!" called the conductor. "The end of the line!"

One by one the passengers filed out. Emily clutched her purse tightly, although she knew it was empty. "Our money is gone as well," admitted Brother Kirby.

Emily admired the ocean of silver grass stretched out in every direction. *Is this what Zion will look like?* she wondered. *Will I ever get there?*

Brother Kirby turned to Emily. "Many of the Union officers are hiring immigrant girls as servants and companions for their wives."

"Please, Brother Kirby, don't make me go. ... I can't go to war. I need to get to Zion."

"Pardon me. Am I to understand this young lady wants to go to the Great Salt Lake City?" spoke a man behind them.

"All three of us," answered Brother Kirby.

"Then to Salt Lake City you shall go! My name's Leatham, and I'm heading a team of freight wagons there. You can herd the cattle, your wife can help cook, and the young lady can follow along, gathering fuel."

There were no other children, and Emily had to earn her keep. On foot.

Emily stared at the butter churn attached to the wagon in front of her. By evening, chunks of butter would be scooped off, squeezed, and eaten for supper. At home, butter was a rare treat, but today the sloshing churn only reminded Emily that she would be served beans and biscuits again.

Around her neck and over one shoulder was slung a cowhide pouch that Emily kept full of buffalo chips and small pieces of wood for kindling. She had grown thin, her face caked with dust, her feet pinched and swollen.

She sat down, unhooked her shoes, and placed them on a rock beside the road. It seemed wrong not to give them to Martha, but perhaps someone else could use them. She rose and continued barefoot down the trail.

From then on, every evening, Emily sat by the campfire and pulled tiny thorns from the bottom of her feet.

It was the hottest day Emily could remember. Sweat rolled down her cheeks, smearing the dust on her face into mud. The trail was steep, and sharp rocks cut through the calluses on her feet. The freight wagons moved more slowly than ever, and the wind blew dirt in her eyes.

Emily thought of England and the cool grass of home.

Nobody cares if I live or die.

I'm tired and I don't want to walk anymore.

She stopped.

"I'm not taking another step!" Emily cried out loud.

She plunked down on a large flat rock and watched the wagons roll on.

Without her.

All around her was silence. A coyote howled in the distance, and Emily sprang from the rock like a startled deer. She ran and ran, tripping over stones, ignoring the pain in her feet.

Supper was cleaned up and all were in bed. Emily had not been missed. She crawled under one of the wagons and prayed, *Father in Heaven, I am so weary and dirty and alone. I don't want to go to Zion anymore. I just want to go home.*

A cool breeze tempered the heat the next morning as Emily limped along. Thoughts of England or Salt Lake failed to ease her pain. Both seemed too far away.

But then something moved on her side of the road, and Emily quickened her pace. Lying on the ground like a worn blanket was a white ox—sickly, weak, and left to die.

Emily raced to the food wagon, ladled some water into a bowl, and returned. Gently she raised the ox's head and held the bowl under his chin. Then she gathered some grass and knelt beside him as he chewed it.

"Don't worry, old fellow, I'll take care of you," she whispered.

To her surprise, the ox rose to his feet. Emily picked up the rope that hung around his neck and led him down the trail.

ach morning, Emily woke early to water her ox. She kept her hands full of sweet grass and sang softly to him. Each night she lay close to him and stroked his nose until she fell asleep.

The days passed quickly, and the ox grew stronger until Emily could ride on his back.

She no longer wondered how far it was to Zion.

On Emily's eleventh birthday, October 10, 1863, the wagon
train arrived in Salt Lake City.
Riders had been sent ahead, and a crowd gathered to meet them.
Emily dropped her rope and ran to her uncle John.

She told him all about her journey—the ship,
the freight cars, Captain Leatham.
And her white ox.
Emily turned to the wagons but did not see
her friend. *I can't lose him.*

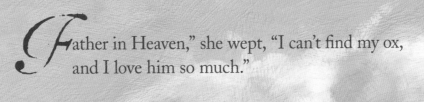

"Father in Heaven," she wept, "I can't find my ox, and I love him so much."

A soft wind cooled her tears, and Emily felt calm.
    She scanned the horizon to see the Rocky Mountains surrounding her like a warm blanket. "I believe my ox was sent to help me reach Zion, and now he's gone to someone who needs him more than I do."
    She took Uncle John's hand. Finally, Emily was home.

afterword Emily's mother, with John and Martha, joined Emily in Salt Lake City in 1866. Eventually Emily married John Squires, a widower. She helped raise his five children as well as ten of her own. She lived a life of faith and devotion and of love and compassion—in the Salt Lake Valley.

As she grew old, Emily would hold her grandchildren close and tell them of her journey to Utah, especially of her friend, the white ox, whom she believed God had sent to comfort and strengthen her.

This story was adapted from "The Child's Journey," written by Laura Squires Robinson and published in *Hidden Treasures of Pioneer History*, a collection of stories about the early settlers of Utah, and from family histories written by Virginia Bryan and Jasmine Arnold, granddaughters of Emily Swain Squires.